D1646977

IMAGINE THAT™
Licensed exclusively to Imagine That Publishing Ltd
Tide Mill Way, Woodbridge, Suffolk, IP12 1AP, UK
www.imaginethat.com

2 4 6 8 9 7 5 3
Manufactured in China

Written by Nat Lambert
Illustrated by Rosie Butcher

ISBN 978-1-78958-449-3

A catalogue record for this book is available from the British Library

Goldilocks and the three bears

Written by Nat Lambert
Illustrated by Rosie Butcher

Once upon a time, there were three bears;
Daddy Bear, Mummy Bear and Baby Bear.
Every morning the three bears all ate a bowl
of delicious porridge for breakfast.

One day, the three bears went for a walk in the forest to let their porridge cool down.

Meanwhile, a little girl called Goldilocks was playing in the forest. As she passed by the three bears' cottage, Goldilocks smelt something delicious coming from inside.

Goldilocks was hungry, so she peeped through the window and saw three bowls of porridge on the table.

'Mmm, that porridge looks very tasty,' she said, and crept into the cottage.

First, Goldilocks took a spoonful of porridge from the largest bowl.

'Ouch!' she squealed.
'This porridge is far too hot!'

Next, Goldilocks took a spoonful from the medium-sized bowl of porridge.

'Yuck!' she said. ***'This porridge is far too cold!'***

Finally, Goldilocks took a spoonful from the smallest bowl of porridge.

'Mmm, this porridge is just right!'

So Goldilocks ate all of the porridge and even licked the bowl clean!

Now that Goldilocks wasn't hungry any more, she began to explore the rest of the cottage. First, she wandered into the living room where she saw three chairs.

First, Goldilocks sat down on the largest chair.

'Ouch! This chair is much too hard!' she grumbled.

Goldilocks then sat down on the medium-sized chair.

'Oh dear, this chair is much too soft,' she said.

Finally, Goldilocks sat down on the smallest chair.

'This chair is perfect!' smiled Goldilocks.

Goldilocks rocked back and forth until, suddenly, there was a loud cracking noise and the little chair collapsed beneath her!

Goldilocks tried to put the chair back together again, but it was well and truly broken. So, she quickly left the living room and went upstairs.

In the bedroom, Goldilocks found three beds. She let out a huge yawn; it had been a busy day, and she was tired.

Goldilocks decided to try the biggest bed.

'Ouch! This bed is much too hard!' she complained.

Next, she tried the medium-sized bed.

'Oh dear! This bed is much too soft!' she said.

Finally, Goldilocks tried the smallest bed.

'This bed is perfect!' she sighed, as she snuggled down under the covers and fell fast asleep.

A little while later the three bears arrived home from their walk.

They were glad to be home again and were looking forward to their breakfast.

'Who's been eating my porridge?'

growled Daddy Bear.

'Who's been eating my porridge?'

said Mummy Bear.

'And who's been eating my porridge? It's all gone!'

cried Baby Bear.

The three puzzled, hungry bears went into the living room to sit down.

'Who's been sitting in my chair?'

growled Daddy Bear.

'Who's been sitting in my chair?'

cried Mummy Bear.

'And who's been sitting in my chair? It's broken!'

sobbed Baby Bear.

The three bears were very upset that someone had been in the house, so they went upstairs to look around.

'Who's been sleeping in my bed?'

growled Daddy Bear.

'Who's been sleeping in my bed?'

gasped Mummy Bear.

'And who's been sleeping in my bed ... and is still there?'

whispered Baby Bear.

Just then, Goldilocks woke up and saw the three bears standing over her. She screamed loudly, leapt out of bed, and ran as fast as she could, all the way home.

'I don't think she'll go into someone's house without being invited ever again!' laughed Daddy Bear.

'Now, let's make some more porridge!'